THE DEVIL IN ROOM 13

ASTOR ALPHAS

CLARA KING

1

———

ALICE

"AND THE OSCAR GOES TO ... Alice Mulligan!"

The crowd erupts into applause, filling the theater with whistles and shrieks of glee. My husband beams from beside me and pulls me toward him, crushing his lips against mine until it feels like we're the only people in the room. His warm mouth melts me in his arms before he draws back and murmurs in my ear, "I'm so proud of you, Alice. I can't believe you won your seventh Oscar!"

I smile bashfully and rise from my seat, waving at the audience as I ascend the steps to the stage. The crowd is on its feet, staring at me in awe.

"Alice! Alice! Alice!" they cheer.

"Alice!" The unwelcome voice startles me from my reverie, and the theater dissolves before my eyes until I'm back to reality, standing in a supply room at the Astor Hotel. I whip around toward the voice, and my stomach sinks as I see my boss marching down the corridor toward me. Her face is pinched with irritation. "Were you daydreaming again?"

Dammit.

"No," I reply a little too quickly.

Cynthia stares down at me, her hands on her hips. I cower beneath her gaze. She's wearing her signature scowl: pursed lips curved downward, thin eyebrows creased into a frown, and narrowed eyes shooting death rays in my direction. She looks even more hostile than usual today. *How is that even possible?*

Her voice goes dangerously quiet as she says, "This is the third time this week that I've caught you staring into space doing nothing. Do I need to remind you that this is your probationary period? Your future at the Astor relies on your work this month."

"No, you don't need to remind me. I'm sorry, Cynthia. I'll do better."

She turns her nose up at me and snaps, "I'll believe that when I see it. Now, room 4 needs extra towels. Get on it, stat!" She barks the final word like an order.

Embarrassed, I scurry deeper into the supply room, searching for the towels among rows of folded white bathrobes and floor mats. Everything looks identical in here.

Cynthia watches me from the doorway, her eyes burning into the back of my head. Heat rises to my cheeks. *Where are the damn towels?*

With a flood of relief, I finally see a pile of them in the corner, and I frantically gather them up in my arms. I try to dash past Cynthia, but one of her black high-heeled shoes slides out, tripping me. I land hard on the floor.

She tuts. "Clumsiness will not be tolerated at the Astor."

"But you tripped me!" I cry, rubbing my sore hip.

"Lies are not tolerated either," she says, glowering at me. "There will be severe consequences next time."

I pick up the towels from the floor, and Cynthia's bony hand shoots out, grabbing my wrist. "What do you think you're doing?"

"I'm taking the towels. You just asked me—"

"Do you think that's an acceptable standard for the Astor? Put those in the laundry and get some fresh towels that haven't been on the floor. And don't drop them again!"

She turns away, muttering "useless girl" under her breath. I want to scream. But instead, I take a deep breath and grab a new set of towels before heading toward room 4.

I plaster a smile on my face for the guests I pass in the hallway, but rage is prickling under my skin. The day has barely begun and I already want it to be over. Tears of frustration are welling up behind my eyes. *Just another day at the Astor.*

My job here is nothing like I was expecting it to be. When I first applied to be a room service attendant, the Astor seemed like a dream come true. It's a luxury country hotel nestled in Vermont's Green Mountains, complete with a spa, swimming pool, golf course, and even its own private ski slopes. I spent hours staring at photos of the hotel's beamed ceilings and roaring fireplaces, daydreaming about my dazzling new life at the Astor. Sure, I knew I'd have to work hard, but I expected to meet lots of cool people on the job. *How wrong I was.*

In reality, I run backward and forward all day, pushing an insanely heavy service cart around a maze of rooms, all while trying not to knock anybody over. Most of my human interaction comes from being yelled at by Cynthia, except for some brief snatches of conversation when I deliver meals to the guests. But even then, I have to put on my perkiest voice and follow the Astor-approved script: "Are you enjoying your stay?", "Can I get you anything else?", "Have a great day!". Nobody wants to stay and talk to the room service girl. They want me to take my tip and go away as fast as possible.

No wonder I've been daydreaming so often—my fantasies are much more appealing than reality right now —but I desperately need the money, and in rural Vermont, my options are pretty limited. So, I've resolved to simply grin and bear it until I can find somewhere else to work.

I hand the fresh towels to the guest in room 4—who shuts the door in my face without a thank you—before weaving my way through the oak-paneled hallway toward the elevator. I give myself a quick once-over in the mirror as the elevator descends. Cynthia loves to harp on about the importance of looking professional.

I run one hand through my long brown hair, trying

to untangle the knots while using the other hand to brush down my uniform. It's a maid's outfit: a short-sleeved black dress with a white collar and an apron with large pockets. As usual, some of my cat's stubborn hairs stick to the material, but before I can start picking them off, the elevator doors open. Jade stands in the hallway, looking unusually harried.

"Alice!" she exclaims. "There you are."

Jade is the closest thing I have to a friend at the Astor. She works at reception, so our paths don't cross much at work, but we always chat during our lunch break. Well, Jade does most of the chatting. She loves to talk. And as a forty-year-old single mom to three kids, it takes a lot to ruffle Jade's feathers, so her tense expression worries me.

"Is everything okay?" I ask, frowning. Jade doesn't reply but beckons me to follow her.

"Cynthia sent me to round up as many people as I can. She wants to talk to us."

Oh no, I think. *This can't be good.* "About what?"

"I'm not sure, but she looks weird," Jade says. "You'll see in a minute."

Intrigued, I follow Jade. We push through the double doors into the hotel kitchen, where every surface shines with steel appliances. The usual chaos of the breakfast rush is missing. Instead, the hotel employees stand around murmuring and looking impatient. Facing the crowd is Cynthia. She turns to look at Jade and me as we walk in, but instead of her usual scowl, there is a wild look in her eyes. She looks petrified.

"Cynthia, it's the breakfast rush," one of the chefs says. "Our customers are waiting."

"Quiet!" Cynthia calls, a feverish edge to her voice. "This won't take long." The crowd hushes, and we all stare as her face morphs into a bizarre, fake smile. "I've just received a call from Mark Astor's assistant in New York … he's coming to stay here at the Astor." Her voice wavers, and we all stare at her blankly, a few people still murmuring about the breakfast rush.

"Who's Mark Astor?" asks Nick, one of the servers.

"Mark Astor is the billionaire who owns the Astor Hotel chain, including this hotel," she snaps. "He's the son of Dario Astor, the chain's founder. You might know all this if you opened a book every once in a while."

The crowd ignores her rudeness—we're pretty damn used to it by now—but people start to perk up at the word billionaire.

"When is he coming?" somebody asks.

"11:30."

Our heads collectively swivel toward the clock on the kitchen wall.

"That's only three hours away!" someone else yelps.

"That is why I've called you all here," Cynthia says. Her eyes are still wide and fearful, but her tone has reverted to its usual sneering coldness. "Mark Astor owns this place and everything in it, and he has the power to shut us down. You should treat his arrival like an inspection. Every detail must be perfect: his meals, his service, his facilities, his spa experience, everything."

"Why would he want to shut us down?" Jade asks from beside me.

Cynthia's focus snaps to Jade like a bird of prey spotting a mouse. "I doubt any of you have the mental capacity to understand complicated financial matters. But as I've tried to explain on numerous occasions, this hotel is severely underperforming. You are not doing enough," she says, surveying the crowd with a withering look.

There are splutters of disagreement from every corner of the kitchen, which Cynthia silences with a loud clap of her hands. "It's no good trying to argue with the facts. Our profits are not high enough, and it's down to lazy service. Mark Astor's visit is a chance for all of you to prove that this hotel is worth the money and investment that goes into it. You cannot afford to make a single mistake. Do you understand me?"

Her narrowed eyes rest on me for a moment longer than anyone else when she says this, and I quickly look away.

She turns on her heel and leaves the room, the crowd muttering angrily in her wake. In the space of a moment, the kitchen returns to its usual chaotic state. The chefs start on breakfast and everyone else races back to work. I start stacking a service cart with as many breakfast items as I can fit, already daydreaming about how I wish I could have handled that situation.

"We are doing enough, Cynthia!" I would say firmly, my gaze fierce. "You're the one holding this place back with

your horrible attitude and mean personality. We don't want you here anymore. Get out and never come back!" The crowd would clap and cheer, and Cynthia would grovel at my feet, begging for forgiveness.

Maybe this Mark Astor guy will see how awful she is and fire her. The idea makes me smile to myself, but I doubt I'll be that lucky. I bet Mark Astor is a grouchy old snob who's never satisfied with anything and spends all day playing golf with his equally snooty buddies. He'll probably love Cynthia and tell her to work us all even harder. I shake away this incredibly annoying thought and get back to work.

BY THE TIME 11:15 a.m. comes around, I'm getting curious. Mark Astor is due to arrive in fifteen minutes, and I'm clearly not the only one who's interested. Several other employees dawdle in the lobby and take their time walking past the reception desk, their eyes darting frequently toward the front doors. There's a strange excitement buzzing in the air, a sense of anticipation as we await Mark Astor's grand entrance.

By 11:30 a.m., all subtlety is gone: several of us stand around openly staring at the doors, waiting. It looks like something out of Downton Abbey: the household servants waiting to greet their master on his return home.

Soon enough, I notice Cynthia heading our way. I dart behind a large floor plant to hide myself from view, peering out through the plastic leaves to keep the front doors in sight. She doesn't even seem to notice all the employees standing around. She's too busy muttering to herself, her eyes the size of saucers. At 11:45 a.m. we finally hear a car crunch on the gravel outside, and Cynthia gives a strangled squeal that makes us all jump.

It sounds like Mark Astor has arrived.

2

———

MARK

IF I HAD it my way, I would turn around and drive straight back to New York. Being away from the office for an entire week to stay at a hotel in rural Vermont is not my idea of being productive. But this hotel isn't performing as I want it to. I need to see what the problem is and cut out the deadwood.

My company took a risk opening an Astor in such a remote location: most of our hotels are based in major cities like London, Paris, Tokyo ... not fucking Lamoille County, Vermont. My brother Daniel, the Astor's Chief Financial officer, thinks keeping this place open is a mistake. But I don't make mistakes, and I know this place has potential. I'm here to find it, even if I'd much rather be in my office with a view of Manhattan's soaring skyline and an urgent deadline to meet.

I get restless when I'm not at work. I need purpose. I need to achieve.

Are you ready to work harder than yesterday?

That was my dad's motto when he was alive. He was the most hardworking man I've ever known. What started as a couple of family-run hotels in upstate New York—barely worth a dime each—grew into a billion-dollar chain of luxury hotels around the world, and it was all down to my dad's perseverance. But he's gone now. It's up to me to continue his success and expand on it. I'm determined to turn the billion-dollar Astor chain into the biggest hotel empire in the world and make my dad proud, even if he's not here to see it. Every day is a step closer to my goal, and I won't let this shit set me back. I'm going to find the problem here and fix it, even if I'd much rather be elsewhere.

With some reluctance, I step out of the warmth of my Bugatti and into Vermont's crisp October air, dragging my suitcase behind me. Even a city man like me has to admit that fall is pretty damn impressive out here: the trees are ablaze with the most vivid red and orange leaves I've ever seen. It looks like a painting. The Astor looms ahead, a sprawling white hotel with more windows than I can count, nestled against a backdrop of mountains. I stride up the steps toward the glass front doors and head inside.

There's a whole fucking welcoming committee. Astor employees ogle me from every corner of the lobby, all trying to get a good look at the bigshot CEO, no doubt. I survey them, unimpressed. No wonder this hotel is going to shit—all the employees are standing around staring at me instead of looking after guests. One of them walks hesitantly toward me—a middle-aged woman with a down-turned mouth and a look of complete terror on her face. I watch her blankly. Why is this lady staring at me like I'm an axe murderer?

"Can I help you?" I ask, raising an eyebrow at her.

"Oh, Mr. Astor!" she exclaims breathlessly. "It's such an honor to have you here. I'm Cynthia Ratcliff, the hotel manager." She wrings my hand, still looking at me like I just threatened to kill her whole family.

I give her a curt nod. "I'd like to be shown to my room."

"Yes, of course! Of course, of course ..." her voice trails off, and she spins around looking flustered. "Someone take Mr. Astor's bags to room 13. Stat!" She shouts the last word right next to my damn ear. "And the rest of you, get back to work!"

The curious employees slowly begin to disperse. All except one. I can see someone peering at me from behind a large potted plant near the front desk. I'm getting pretty sick of being stared at in my own hotel, and I walk toward the figure, crossing my arms.

"Enjoying the show?" I ask.

The figure freezes before slowly creeping out from behind the plant to reveal ... the most beautiful girl I've ever seen in my whole damn life. I feel like I've been hit by a fucking bus. It takes me a moment to recover as I take her in: her big brown eyes framed by thick lashes, a smattering of freckles on her nose, pillowy lips slightly parted. My eyes roam her body—her full breasts straining against her dress, her wide hips, and the smooth, pale skin of her bare legs. I can picture those legs spread wide apart, inviting me in, and I feel my cock start to swell for the first time in forever.

The girl looks mortified to have been caught spying. Her cheeks redden as she looks down at the floor, adorably shame-faced.

"ALICE MULLIGAN!" Cynthia shouts, following my line of vision and clapping eyes on the girl. "That's the second time today I've caught you shirking your responsibilities." Cynthia's face is no longer scared. It's contorted with rage. She looks livid. "You're absolutely useless. You're fired! And don't expect a reference from us."

She stops her tirade with a deep breath and turns back to me, immediately switching back to reverence. "I'm so sorry about that, Mr. Astor. This was her probationary period, and she's proven many times that she's not fit to join our staff."

I look at Alice, her trembling lips, tears pooling in her eyes, and I see red. Anger ignites my veins and I round on Cynthia.

"There were about twenty people in here doing nothing when I came in," I snap. "You didn't fire any of them. I won't tolerate unfair treatment in my hotels, and if I see any more evidence of it, you'll be the one getting fired."

Her jaw drops. "I-I ..." she stammers, unable to continue.

I glower at her before turning back to Alice. "Don't cry," I say, desperately wishing I could draw her into my arms and kiss her tears away. "You're not fired. I won't allow it. Ever."

Alice gives me a watery smile, and I want to pick her up and carry her to room 13, where I can truly make her mine. I want to see that beautiful face flushed with pleasure, her mouth open in a scream she can't hold back as I push inside her, claiming her for my own. I feel my cock twitch, the hardness of it pressing tightly against my pants. God, this girl is killing me. I want her. And I always get what I want.

"Show me to room 13, Alice," I say, fighting to keep my voice steady as I fix my eyes on hers. Alice shoots Cynthia a look of uncertainty, like she's asking for her permission. I shake my head. "You will do as I say. I'm your boss, not her, understand?"

Alice bites her lip. "Yes, Mr. Astor."

"Mark."

"Yes, Mark," she repeats, grabbing a keycard from behind the front desk and leading me toward room 13. My skin tightens when she says "Mark" in that sweet little voice. *I can come up with far more exciting ways to make her say my name,* I think, as I follow her through the hallways.

Her plump, round ass cheeks bounce slightly as she walks, begging to be squeezed and spanked. *God, she's perfect.* I can't tear my eyes away from her, and my chest stirs with unfamiliar desires: I want to protect her, keep her safe, claim every inch of her. I never used to believe in love at first sight, but fuck, Alice has made a believer out of me. This girl is mine. And if she doesn't know it yet, then she will soon enough.

3

ALICE

MY FACE IS STILL BURNING as I lead Mark to his room. Being caught staring at him from behind a plant was humiliating enough, but to get fired straight afterward? I'm mortified. My nerves are still frazzled when I remember Cynthia's fury and her hate-filled voice when she called me useless. But Mark stood up for me, and I am so grateful that he let me keep my job despite everything Cynthia said.

He's definitely not the grouchy old man I was expecting. My heart was practically in my throat when I first saw him walk in: his piercing blue eyes and luscious dark hair captivated me instantly, not to mention his jawline, which could probably cut through a diamond. I can hear his heavy footsteps right behind me, making me shiver a little as I think of his hulking height and broad chest and the way his muscles strain against his pristine white dress shirt. I want to turn and face him, drinking him in all over again, but I keep walking until we're finally outside room 13.

"Here you go." I hand him the keycard. He takes it from me, his large hand dwarfing my own as our fingers brush lightly, sending another shiver down my spine. I compose myself and say, "Thank you, by the way. For standing up for me and letting me keep my job."

I look up at him, trying to muster a sincere smile, but his eyes make my breath catch. The intense blue is mesmerizing, but I'm more struck by the longing in his gaze. He looks like he's just found water in a desert. The world falls away until there is only Mark and me, lost in each other's eyes. *What is happening?*

"You don't need to thank me," he says.

God, I could get used to that deep, gravelly voice. I'm desperate to hear him say my name.

"Cynthia doesn't like me getting distracted. I daydream sometimes when I'm not too busy. But I work hard, honestly!" I feel a sudden need to impress him—to make sure he doesn't think I really am useless. But it's also the truth. I do work hard at the Astor, no matter what Cynthia says about my daydreaming. I'm sore and exhausted every night when my shift is over.

"What do you daydream about?" he asks huskily, his face just inches from mine.

My heart stutters. *Your tongue between my legs,* I think.

"All sorts of things. In high school, my teachers called me Alice in Wonderland because I was always lost in fantasy worlds," I say with a giggle. "Today, I daydreamed about winning an Oscar, and my husband kissing me in front of the whole audience." I regret the words as soon as they leave my mouth. *Stop talking, you sound ridiculous,* I think.

Mark is frowning. "Husband?" he asks, his voice lowering to a growl. "You have a husband?"

"No! No, not at all. It was just in the daydream."

"A boyfriend, then?" The thought seems to spark something feral in his eyes, and a thrill of excitement shoots from the back of my neck, right down to my toes.

"No, never. And you, is there a Mrs. Astor?" I ask, trying to smile even though the thought of this man belonging to somebody else fills me with a sinking dread I can't explain.

I see the corner of his mouth tug into a smirk. "Not yet," he says, his eyes drifting down my body and back up to my mouth. "But I've got my eye on someone."

"Ahem!" Someone clears their throat loudly and I whip around to see Cynthia glowering at me from the end of the hallway, her arms crossed. "Alice, get back to work. The lunch rush is coming up."

I obey her automatically, turning toward the kitchen, but Mark grabs my wrist. The vise-like contact makes my heart skip.

"She'll go back to work if and when I say," Mark sneers. "This is my fucking hotel."

"This may be your hotel, Mr. Astor," Cynthia replies, her voice wavering slightly, "But I am the hotel manager, and I'm responsible for the employees we have here. I will not tolerate Alice avoiding her responsibilities."

Her voice sounds measured and reasonable, but then she shoots me a look of disgust so withering that I feel myself flinch. Mark sees it and clenches his jaw. He strides toward her, his face livid. "Now, you listen to me, Cynthia. This is the second time you've crossed me today. There will not be a third. If you so much as look at Alice the wrong way ever again, I will not only fire your ass, but I'll make sure no hotel will ever hire you again. Do you understand?"

My heart thumps at his words. *He's protecting me.*

Cynthia scowls at him, but I can see she's scared of his threat. "Fine, Mr. Astor. Do whatever you like. Alice, if you think your overworked colleagues can handle the lunch rush without you, then by all means, stand around all day and do nothing. Now, if you don't mind, I have a job to do." She turns on her heel and marches away.

Her words fill me with shame. I never thought I'd say it, but Cynthia's right: it's not fair for the other girls to handle lunch on their own while I stand around talking to a gorgeous billionaire.

"I really should get back to work, Mr. Astor," I say reluctantly. "There's a lot to do."

Mark shakes his head. "Don't go back to work."

"But—"

"Please," he says gruffly. "Don't go back to work. Come inside with me." He leans toward me and for a second, I think he's about to kiss me. But at that moment, a ringtone blares from his pocket. "Fuck," he mutters. "Ignore that."

"You can answer it," I tell him. "I don't mind." But Mark declines the call and turns his gaze back to me, his eyes swimming with lust.

"Alice, I want—" The ringtone sounds again. "Fuck!"

Mark turns away from me and pulls the phone out of his pocket, glaring at the screen. I use the distraction to slink away unnoticed, hurrying quietly down the hallway and shutting myself in a nearby supply closet.

I wanted to say yes. *Yes, yes, yes, I will come inside with you.* The offer was unbearably tempting, but I know I have to be practical. It's not just the lunch rush that's worrying me. Mark is only booked in at the Astor for a week, and after that, he'll go back to his office in New York. He'll meet a supermodel heiress, and they'll live happily ever after in some luxury apartment in Manhattan, and I'll never see him again. That's the kind of woman Mark Astor is destined for. Not a room service attendant from the middle of nowhere who spends her days wheeling meals around a hotel. The thought makes my stomach drop.

Plus, when he leaves, Cynthia will go back to being my only boss. Then I'll really be in trouble. I can't afford to lose this job, and I need to pull my weight to stay on her good side.

But more importantly, I need to keep my heart safe. If I let myself fall for Mark, I know I won't be able to bear the pain of him leaving next week. It would break me, and no matter how badly I want to forget all of that and go straight back to him, I can't. I have to be sensible. I have to protect myself. But damn, it's not easy.

I don't want to cower in a supply closet feeling sorry for myself all day. Instead, I slip into a daydream, imagining Mark's mouth on mine, the heat of his tongue, the pressure of his chest against me. Desire burns in my core. I wish more than anything that I could let him have his naughty way with me in room 13. I wish I didn't care about the consequences. But I do. So instead, I crouch behind the shelves of the supply closet, pull up my dress, and slip my hand in my panties, teasing open my wet folds. I'm slick with desire, and I rub my swollen clit in circles until I'm breathless, going faster and faster. I imagine that it's Mark's tongue licking me roughly, relentlessly, his breath warm against my most intimate area. My pussy clenches tight and throbs with release as I gasp his name.

Mark. Mark. Mark.

Even after my orgasm, the aching need between my legs doesn't subside. I groan in frustration and pull my dress back down before peeking out of the supply closet to make sure Mark isn't nearby. Feeling a mixture of relief and disappointment when I don't see him, I head toward the kitchen to prepare for the lunch rush, wishing I was in room 13 instead.

4

———

MARK

I ONLY LOOKED AWAY for a second. I was trying to put my damn phone on silent to stop it from disturbing us again, but when I turned back around, Alice was already gone. Fuck! Now I'm racing through the hallways, desperately searching for her, but all the doors are closed and she's nowhere to be seen. I just found the girl of my dreams and I've lost her already. I'm fucking furious with myself.

My phone starts to vibrate in my pocket again, and I wrench it out.

"WHAT?" I shout into the phone.

"Woah, calm down," says Daniel, my brother. "It's me—I'm just calling to check how it's going up in Vermont."

"You called me like five fucking times. I was in the middle of something important." I continue storming around the hallways, my phone to my ear as I hunt for my girl like a dog sniffing out a scent.

"Three times, dickhead," Daniel corrects "If you answered your damn phone, I would only need to call you once."

"What do you want?" I snap. It's not my brother's fault that Alice is gone, but being without her is making me fucking agitated.

"I just told you; I called to see how it's going up there. What's the deal with this shitty hotel? Have you figured out why they're having all these problems?"

I haven't been thinking about the hotel at all. Work hasn't crossed my mind since I got here, which is a first for me. Meeting Alice has driven everything else from my head, and suddenly, figuring out what's wrong with this hotel seems like the least important thing in the world. All that matters is finding Alice.

"I don't know yet," I say. "I only just arrived. When I get some updates, I'll call you." I already know damn well I'm not going to call him.

"I just can't figure out where all the money is going. Our budget is fucking huge for that hotel. There should be plenty of staff, state-of-the-art facilities—the place should be raking in the dough. Instead, they're under-staffed, overworked, and struggling to break even from what I hear."

"I'll look into it," I say distractedly, as I peer down yet another empty corridor.

"Well, get on it, buddy! You only have a week out there."

I end the call, ignoring Daniel's warning and turning

the damn phone off for good measure. I don't want any more distractions.

After walking all around the hotel, from the spa to the restaurant, I've somehow circled back to room 13. This place is like a fucking maze, and I haven't found Alice delivering lunch anywhere. I'm prepared to turn this place upside down if that's what it takes.

Then I'm struck by a worrying thought: Cynthia. *Fuck.* If she finds Alice without me there to protect her, what will she do to her? My head conjures an image of Cynthia shouting, her eyes crazed, her hand whipping forward to slap Alice's soft cheek. I know I'm being dramatic—I doubt Cynthia would risk her job so carelessly—but as long as there is someone in this hotel with a grudge against my girl, I can't rest easy.

From the moment I set eyes on that bitch hotel manager, I've had a bad feeling about her in my gut. It's not just her vicious attitude toward Alice that bothers me, it's the way she looked at me when I first entered the building—her fearful expression when we met. She looked like a woman with something to hide.

"Where is Cynthia Ratcliff's office?" I ask a passing room attendant.

"In the lobby, sir. Behind the front desk."

I barely have time to mutter my thanks before racing back the way I came.

I BARGE into Cynthia's office without knocking, and she looks up from her computer, bewildered. There's panic in her eyes when she realizes it's me. I watch as she frantically closes something on her screen, trying and failing to do it subtly. She looks back up at me, smoothing her features into a smile that doesn't reach her eyes.

"How can I help you, Mr. Astor?"

"Where's Alice?"

"I have no idea," she says, her lip curling. "Standing around daydreaming somewhere, I imagine. As usual." *I've had just about enough of this bitch.*

"You're up to something, Cynthia," I say, glowering at her. The fear is back in her gaze. "I'm going to find out what it is, and when I do, you're through."

"I don't know what you're talking about." Her worried expression convinces me I'm right.

"I think you do. I could fire you right now, but I'll have much more fun uncovering all your secrets first. You're going to regret treating Alice like shit." I don't wait for her to reply. I storm out of her office and slam the door behind me.

That bitch can't be trusted. I'm going to take great pleasure in finding out her dirty little secrets and taking her down, making sure Alice never has to see her again. But confirming my doubts about Cynthia hasn't fixed my main problem: where the hell is Alice?

I resolve to head for the kitchen and wait for her to show up there when suddenly, a better idea strikes me. *Of course!* I want to kick myself for being a fucking idiot and not thinking of it before.

Back outside room 13, I let myself in with the key card and close the door. My room is impressive, boasting a roaring fireplace and a beautiful view of the fiery red and gold forest outside. But more importantly, there's an enormous four-poster bed. I can already picture Alice squirming on that thick mattress, clawing at the sheets in pleasure. I shake myself from my thoughts and reach straight for the hotel phone, dialing the number listed for room service. The call connects.

"Hello, this is room service. Can I please take your order?" a man says.

"I want a bottle of champagne brought up to me right away," I demand. "And I want it delivered by Alice Mulligan. Tell her that if she's not here in five minutes, I'll come and carry her to room 13 myself."

THE LUNCH RUSH is insane today. I've barely had a moment to breathe. After racing around the hotel like a crazy person, I'm finally back in the kitchen restocking the lunch cart when someone taps me on the shoulder. I turn to see Nick, one of the servers, holding out a bottle of champagne.

"This is for room 13."

My breath catches when he says the room number. *Mark.* "But-but I'm still doing this cart," I stammer.

"I'll get someone else to do it," Nick says. "Room 13 is Mr. Astor's room, and he's our top priority. He asked for you specifically, by name, and he wants it in under five minutes. Otherwise, he said something about coming to get you himself."

If Nick finds this strange, he thankfully doesn't mention it. Instead, he eyes me impatiently, waiting for me to take the bottle, which I do.

My legs have turned to Jell-O as I leave the kitchen

and head back toward Mark's room. *I was trying so hard to be practical ... avoid heartache ... yet here I am, walking straight back toward it. Nice one, Alice.*

I reach room 13 and raise my hand to knock. My fist has barely touched the wood when the door is flung open.

Mark stands before me with his shirt unbuttoned, looking unbearably handsome. I open my mouth to say something, but he doesn't wait to hear it. He leans down and crushes his lips to mine, pushing me back against the wall of the hallway. I moan as the weight of his body presses against me, his warm tongue sliding into my mouth, dominating mine. I feel his rock-hard cock pushing against my abdomen and heat pools between my legs, filling me with an unbearable ache.

God, I want him so badly.

He pulls away, leaving me desperate for more.

"Why did you leave?" he asks urgently.

I'm too embarrassed to tell him about my fears of heartbreak. What if he doesn't feel the same? What if this is all just a game to him? A little fun on the side while he's away from work? The thought makes me clam up. I can't tell him how I feel, so I focus on my fears about work instead.

"I really need to keep this job. Cynthia will fire me for sure if I don't work super hard today." It feels like I'm lying to him. I wish I could tell him the real reasons why I can't stay with him, but I can't risk the pain of rejection.

"Alice, I promise you I won't let her mistreat you ever

again." Mark bends down and rests his forehead against mine. "Say the word and I'll make her leave."

"But you won't always be here to take care of things."

"I will always take care of you," he says fiercely. "Do you understand?"

He pulls me into his arms and guides me into room 13, shutting the door behind us. Doubts are still echoing inside my mind, but as Mark cocoons me against his muscular chest, I feel myself relax into his embrace. The stress of the lunch rush seeps away, and I feel safe. Peaceful. I could happily stay like this forever, inhaling his masculine scent while he wraps himself around me.

"I brought your champagne," I murmur against his bare chest. His skin is warm and taut over his muscles, and I can't resist stroking it.

"Fuck the champagne. It was just an excuse to see you."

My heart floods with warmth, and I look up at him, looping my arms around his neck.

"I'm sorry I ran away," I say. "It wasn't really about my job. I was just scared."

"What are you scared of?" He cups my cheek, his thumb lightly brushing my face.

I should tell him everything: that I don't want him to break my heart, that I know he's going to leave soon, that I can't face giving him every part of me only to lose him straight afterward. But something holds me back. This all feels too good to be true. Things like this don't happen to girls like me, and I still can't convince myself that

Mark isn't stringing me along. I want to trust him, but I don't know how.

Mark notices my silence and his face turns solemn. "I would never hurt you, baby. I'm here to look after you, not hurt you."

Hearing him call me "baby" in his gruff voice sends a shiver of desire through me.

I want him to call me baby with his cock inside me.

The dirty thought makes my breath catch, and the intensity of Mark's gaze hammers at my resolve. *I have to be brave and tell him the truth, even if I'm still scared.* I might regret it later if Mark breaks my heart, but I know I'll regret it even more if I never take a chance on us.

"You're going back to New York next week," I whisper, looking away. "You'll go back to your regular life, and I'll go back to mine, and this will all be over. That's why I can't do this—if I let myself get too close, it will hurt even more to lose you."

Mark studies me, stroking my hair with his large hand and pulling my body closer. "That's not how this is going to work," he says, his face serious. "You're my girl now, Alice, whether you like it or not. Wherever you are is where I'm going to be."

"But what about your company? Your job?" I splutter.

Mark traces my lips with his long fingers, his mouth curving into a sly smirk. "I'll explain all that in a minute when my fingers are in your pussy."

Before I can register what he just said, he scoops me up into his burly arms, making me squeal in shock as I'm lifted off the floor and carried to his bed. He pins me down and plants a warm string of kisses on my neck, making me tip my head back with a sigh of pleasure. My toes curl as he starts to suck the sensitive spot at the base of my throat.

God, yes.

A whimper of pleasure escapes me, and Mark's eyes darken, filling with need. He crushes his mouth to mine in a frenzied, bruising kiss, his hands wandering down to my breasts, massaging them through the fabric of my uniform.

"God, you're so sexy," he says hoarsely in between kisses. "You have no idea how fucking sexy you are." To prove his point, he presses his crotch against mine, letting me feel the rock-hard erection bulging in his pants. The length of him pressing between my legs makes me shudder. It feels so good. I've never been this wet before ... my panties must be drenched.

Mark seems to read my mind. He yanks up my dress and then ... *oh my God, yes.* My hips buck wildly as his hand enters my panties, his fingers dancing around the swollen nub of my clit, teasing me. "Does that feel good, baby?"

"Yes!" I whimper. The aching between my legs is getting stronger. "I need you so badly it hurts." All my sensible thoughts have abandoned me and a raw animal need has taken over.

"Do you need my cock to fill you up and fuck the ache away?" he asks.

I love it when he says dirty things to me—his deep

voice sends ripples of desire through my body. "Yes, please!"

"Soon. First, I'm going to feel you." He runs a finger down my pussy, touching my wetness. I can smell my own sweet arousal filling the air between us. "Damn baby, you're soaking."

He eases two of his long, thick fingers inside me, and I forget how to breathe. My walls stretch around him, and I gasp as he starts to pump his digits in and out, his eyes never leaving mine. His fingers curl upward with each push, hitting a heavenly spot inside me over and over again until I see stars.

"I promised to explain everything when my fingers were in your pussy, so you better be listening," Mark growls. His voice drips with lust as he continues to relentlessly drive his fingers in and out of me. I barely manage a nod, moaning uncontrollably as he picks up the pace. "Fuck my job," he continues, breathing heavily, "and fuck my company. None of it matters if I don't have you. Do you understand?"

"Oh, Mark!" I gasp, his fingers hitting the deepest part of me.

"I've wasted so many years making work my purpose," he says, lowering himself to kiss me, his fingers still moving. "But the moment I saw you, I knew you were my real purpose, Alice. Not hotels, not profits, not chasing billions of dollars. You."

I feel like I might explode with joy. My heart is overflowing, and I want to ask if he means it. I want to know if this is really happening. I'm struggling to believe that this isn't just another one of my daydreams, but I can see in his eyes that he means every word, and I don't think I've ever been happier. He kisses me deeply, and whispers in my ear, "Now, come for me."

"Oh, God!" The pressure between my legs is building. I can feel my orgasm rushing to the surface, and my body writhes like a wild thing around Mark's thick fingers.

"Come, baby," he commands. "Now."

My body obeys him, shaking as the orgasm rocks through me. Stars pop in front of my eyes and there is nothing but blind pleasure, leaving me breathless and quivering. Mark gazes at me as I shiver through the final pulses. He looks awestruck.

"You're so beautiful when you come."

I giggle, still trying to catch my breath as I reach up to stroke his face, my hand caressing the stubble on his jaw. "That was amazing."

"We're only just getting started," he says.

The devious glint in his eye makes me groan with desire. He bends his head to kiss my neck when suddenly, an ear-splitting sound tears through the room. I jump violently, clapping my hands to my ears as the blaring noise assaults my eardrums, making my head pound.

Just my luck, I think. *It's the damn fire alarm.*

6

MARK

THE ALARM SCARES the shit out of me. Pure adrenaline takes over, and I have only one thought: get Alice out. I pull her off the bed and grab her by the hand, flinging open the door to room 13.

The siren shrieks in my ears—it's even louder out here in the hallway. People are everywhere, rushing toward the emergency exits, and I follow them, not letting Alice out of my sight as I drag her with me.

Thankfully, the sound is muffled when we get outside. We join the crowd swarming the parking lot. Everyone stands around looking unsure and shivering in the frigid weather.

"Are you okay?" I ask, pulling Alice toward me. She nods her head and bites her lip, staring with wide eyes at the hotel. I squeeze her hand and say, "I'm sure it's just a false alarm."

She still looks worried. "I just hope everyone gets out

safely," she says, craning her neck like she's looking for somebody. "I think Jade and the rest of the staff are out. But where's Cynthia?"

I scan the crowd, looking for Cynthia's dour expression. But she's nowhere to be found.

"That's a good question."

"Maybe she's gone to her car," Alice suggests, turning to examine the parking lot. She eyes a bright red Lamborghini. "No, she's not there ... maybe she's rounding up guests inside."

I frown. "The Lamborghini is Cynthia's car?"

"Yeah. Nice, right?" Alice says.

Suspicion creeps into my mind. The car looks brand new. *What the fuck?* How can Cynthia afford a million-dollar Lamborghini?

Speak of the devil. At that moment, Cynthia descends the hotel's front steps. The alarm inside stops, leaving only a ringing in my ears.

"I'm so sorry about that everybody," Cynthia calls. "There's no fire. Our alarm system seems to have malfunctioned, but it's been resolved now. You can all re-enter the hotel."

There is a murmur of relief, and everyone files toward the entrance doors. I notice Cynthia surveying the crowd as we enter until her cold eyes finally land on me. There's something like satisfaction on her face, and suddenly, everything clicks.

The hotel. The profits. The alarm. It finally makes sense.

I usher Alice into the warmth of the hotel and guide

her to a remote corner of the lobby in front of an open fireplace. Goosebumps dot her skin, and I rub her arms to warm her up, holding her against me.

"Warmer now?" I ask.

"Yes, thank you." She kisses my cheek, and my heart skips like I'm a fucking school kid. I want to take her back to room 13 and finish what we started, but I'm struggling to relax knowing that Cynthia is slithering around the place. She has to be dealt with.

"I think Cynthia set off that alarm on purpose," I say, lowering my voice.

Alice cocks her head. "What? Why would she do that?"

"I think she wanted to make sure I was out of the hotel, so she could destroy evidence without me catching her."

"What evidence?"

"Financial records. I think she's been stealing from the hotel accounts. And she's worried that I'm onto her." *And she should be worried. I'm going to destroy her.*

Alice's eyes widen. "Seriously?"

I nod. "It explains everything. The budget for this hotel is huge, but where's all that money going? The place is understaffed and the facilities are outdated as hell. It doesn't make sense. The only explanation is that somebody is skimming off the top of the hotel accounts. She's the hotel manager. It has to be her."

Alice's jaw drops. "Holy crap! But you're the CEO—wouldn't you have noticed it before?"

"I don't deal with the finances for each individual

hotel," I explain. "That's all delegated to the hotel managers."

"So, you're saying that we're all being overworked and yelled at for being useless because Cynthia doesn't want to spend money on hiring more staff?" Alice asks. "She wants to buy a Lamborghini instead?" Her fists clench and anger reddens her cheeks. She looks fierce and beautiful, and I can't wait to crush Cynthia with her by my side.

"I'm going to fix it, baby," I say, stroking her flushed cheek. "I'm going to make her pay for treating you like this."

"Are you going to fire her?"

"Something like that ... I have a few things in mind," I say cryptically.

"Then let's go and confront her. Right now!"

I smile at her enthusiasm. "I promise we'll deal with her soon, but first, you need to eat some lunch."

Alice pouts. "Taking down Cynthia is way more important than food right now." Her stomach growls loudly in protest, and she frowns down at it like it's betrayed her.

"Now that's where you're wrong, baby. There's nothing more important than making sure you're taken care of."

"But—"

"No buts. Come on, we're going back to my room. I'm going to order you everything you want."

"Well, I guess I *have* always wanted to try the butterscotch pudding." *God, she's adorable.*

I lift her hand to my lips, kissing it gently. "Whatever my girl wants, she gets."

7

ALICE

I'VE HAD SO many daydreams about staying at the Astor as a guest, but the reality is better than I could have ever imagined. And it's all because of Mark. He's better than any daydream. And he sure wasn't lying about wanting me fed—he's ordered half the menu to our room.

The table is laden with steaming plates of steak, potatoes, chicken, pasta, cookies, and an extra-large butterscotch pudding. It all looks amazing, and I can't wait to taste the meals I've been wheeling around every day. Cynthia never lets staff have food from the kitchen.

"Thank you for getting all this," I say as I tuck into a plate of roast chicken. "It's delicious."

He meets my gaze. "I can think of something that will be more delicious."

"Oh yeah? Like what?" I ask coyly.

He leans forward across the table, his lips brushing

my ear as he whispers, "Your wet pussy when I make you come for me later on."

"Later on? Why not now?"

Mark chuckles. "A little while ago, you wanted to storm into Cynthia's office straight away, remember?"

"Yeah ..." I pout at him.

"Believe me, I would take you right here and now," he says. "It's taking a lot of self-control not to throw you down on my bed again. But I don't want anything else on your mind when I do. I want you focused on me and nothing else. That's why we're going to deal with Cynthia first." His words make me melt.

"Sounds like a good plan. I want her dealt with, too."

A flicker of fury crosses his face as he asks, "Did Cynthia ever hurt you?"

I think back to all the scathing words and sneering looks, flinching at the memories. "Not physically. She's tripped me a few times, on purpose, but she never hit me, if that's what you mean."

Mark takes a steadying breath, like he's trying to calm himself. "And she insults you, too?"

I nod. "She's always saying I'm useless. When you're told every day that you're dumb and worthless and good for nothing, it starts to stick. It's hard to fight back when I believe everything she's saying." The familiar sadness creeps up on me and I suddenly feel deflated.

Why is self-confidence so damn hard?

Mark reaches out and strokes my cheek. "You're not useless, baby. You're perfect. She's a miserable bitch and

I'm going to make her pay for hurting you. I hate that she's made you feel this way."

"She really hates me," I say thickly, my lip trembling. "She thinks I just stand around daydreaming all the time, but it's not true. And when I do daydream, it's not because I'm trying to be lazy. It's an escape."

"An escape from Cynthia?"

"An escape from everything! In my daydreams, I can be anybody I want to be. I can tame lions in Tanzania, or be a medieval princess, or fly to Jupiter!" I exclaim. "There are no limits. In my daydreams, I'm not just some broke twenty-two-year-old working a lousy job with a boss who hates me. I'm so much more."

Mark gets up from the table and pulls me into his arms, stroking my hair gently. He kisses my cheek and lifts my chin with his thumb until our eyes meet. "You're enough just as you are, Alice. More than enough. You're everything. And I promise I'm going to make all your dreams come true."

I lean into him, breathing in his manly scent and expensive cologne, and the sadness lifts. He feels like home. He feels safe.

"What about your dreams?" I ask.

He takes his time to respond, frowning in thought. "I never really got the chance to have my own dreams. My dad founded the Astor chain, and when he died, there was never an option for me to do anything else."

"That must have been a lot to live up to."

He nods. "My dad worked hard his whole life, every day, all day. He never relaxed, never stopped ... and then one day it caught up with him. He died of a heart attack when I was nineteen."

I feel a pang in my chest as I squeeze Mark's hand. "I'm so sorry."

"It was a long time ago now. Nearly sixteen years. One day, I was a typical college student and the next day I was in charge of running a billion-dollar company. I'd be lying if I said it wasn't a lot of pressure. But I've always tried to follow my dad's example and work hard."

"What were you studying at college?"

"Economics. I dropped out to take over the business. But economics wasn't my dream either." The flicker of a smile crosses his face. "I was always interested in culinary arts."

"Culinary arts?" I repeat. "You wanted to be a chef?" I can barely contain my shock. Trying to imagine Mark in a chef's hat instead of a business suit is a challenge, but the result is pretty damn sexy.

"I didn't put much thought into it. I knew it was impossible, and I didn't want to waste time on a career I could never have. But the idea of owning a restaurant, building the menu, cooking the food, making everything perfect ... I guess if I were the daydreaming type, that would be my daydream."

"That sounds nice," I say wistfully. "I'd love to taste your cooking,"

"You will," he says. "I'll make us butterscotch pudding every day if that's what you want." He plants a kiss on my head. "I've never told anyone about the chef thing before, you know. Only you. You've changed everything for me, Alice. I've been working my ass off for so long to keep my dad's business alive, but then I saw you. And I knew straight away that you were my real purpose. I don't want to work myself into an early grave like my dad. I don't want to be so busy that I never have time for the woman I love. Meeting you has shown me what's really important."

He kisses me then. It's not frantic or bruising like before, it's slow and gentle like he's savoring every moment. Tears well in my eyes and I pull away from the kiss, resting my forehead against his.

"You've changed things for me too," I say. "I've felt so sad and lost lately. My confidence has been at rock bottom ..." I'm so overcome with emotion I can barely speak. "I let Cynthia make me believe I was useless, and I felt so pathetic letting her get away with it. But then I met you, and you make me feel so safe, so special. You make me feel like I'm worthy of love. I feel like I can take on the whole world with you by my side."

"You could take on the world all by yourself, baby. But you won't ever have to because I'll always be here to protect you. My perfect girl." He cradles my cheek with his hand. "Of course you're worthy of love. And you have my love. You'll have it forever. I love you, Alice. Only you."

"I love you too," I say, dazed with happiness. "I love you so much."

"And to prove how much I love you, I'm going to get Cynthia out of this hotel for good." Mark lowers his voice to a whisper in my ear. "Then I'm going to bring you back here, and I'm going to pin you down on my bed and fuck you until you can't breathe."

Oh, God!

"Then I don't want to wait for a second longer," I say. "Let's confront Cynthia."

Mark smirks, his voice teasing. "You sure you don't want another bit of butterscotch pudding?"

"Screw the butterscotch pudding! I want my real dessert." *And that dessert is Mark's cock pounding me until I scream.*

Without warning, Mark stuffs a hand into my panties, running his finger down my slick folds. "That's my girl. All wet and ready for me." The ache between my legs is unbearable, and I squirm with desire.

"Please, let's go!" I moan. "The sooner we go, the sooner we can have dessert."

"I like your logic, baby."

He takes my hand and we leave room 13, ready to bring Cynthia's world crumbling down.

8

MARK

I'M amazed by my self-control as we leave the room. My beautiful angel is soaking wet, her eyes begging me to fuck her, and my cock is so hard it hurts. Every instinct is telling me to pound her like an animal right here in the hallway. But I force myself to resist. My first time with Alice has to be perfect, not a quickie against a wall with Cynthia's presence looming over us. My girl deserves better.

We walk to Cynthia's office, stopping once we reach the closed door. I take a second to text Daniel so he knows exactly what I want him to do, then I pocket my phone and turn to Alice.

"Are you ready?" I ask.

She looks nervous, but determined. "Ready as I'll ever be." I can't resist leaning down for a quick kiss before I open the door.

Cynthia watches us come in from her desk chair, her eyes narrowing with suspicion.

"Hello again, Mr. Astor. What can I do for you this time?" She says it like I've been harassing her for favors every five seconds. And of course, she doesn't even acknowledge Alice. *Fuck you, Cynthia.*

I open my mouth to say this out loud, but Alice cuts in. "We want to talk to you about the money you've been stealing from the hotel accounts."

I glance at my girl's fierce expression, the confident tilt of her chin as she stares Cynthia down. I'm so fucking proud of her.

Cynthia sneers at her. "Finally found a backbone, have you? I don't have time to entertain the delusions of a girl who pushes around a service cart for a living."

"You can look down your nose at me all you want," Alice says. "It won't change the fact that you're a nasty person and I'm not. You're a thief and a liar, and we know what you've been doing." I squeeze her hand to show that I'm here whenever she needs me to jump in.

My baby is on a roll.

"Do you know how ridiculous you sound right now?" Cynthia snaps. "You sound like a toddler pointing fingers across the playground."

"So you deny it?" I ask.

"Of course I deny it. This hotel is underperforming because of lazy, incompetent staff like dear little Alice here. The service is substandard. That's all there is to it."

"We are not useless!" Alice exclaims, balling her fists with rage. "We work our asses off every day while you saunter around bullying everybody. You're the useless one! You're a useless hotel manager, and you're a criminal as well."

Cynthia's face contorts at the word 'criminal'. Seething with rage, she stands up from her chair and leans across her desk at us. "How dare you call me a criminal?"

"That's exactly what you are," I growl. "A thief, a fraud, and a bully."

"You have no proof! You're spouting lies. I ought to sue you both for defamation of character."

I can see the panic building in her eyes. She knows she's being backed into a corner.

"There will be proof and plenty of it," I say. "When I call the police and tell them what you've been up to, they'll seize your computer and find everything you tried to hide." Cynthia's eyes go wild. "Maybe you managed to get rid of some of the physical evidence during your little fire alarm stunt. But the digital evidence will always be there, no matter how well you think you've hidden it."

Cynthia looks at me, then Alice, then me again, her head swiveling back and forth in a frenzied panic. "You're bluffing. You won't call the police—it would be bad press for the Astor brand. Think of how bad it would make you look."

She's getting desperate now. I seize my chance.

"You're right. It would be very bad press for one of our hotel managers to be arrested. That's why I want to negotiate."

"Negotiate?" Cynthia repeats, her face paling.

"Yes. You know what negotiating is, don't you?" I

snarl. "I'm willing to overlook all the shit you've been doing to avoid involving the police. But only on certain conditions."

"What conditions?"

Oh man, I'm enjoying this.

"The first condition is that you apologize to Alice."

Cynthia's face twists with scorn. "I'm not apologizing to her for anything; she should be apologizing to me for being such a crappy employee." Fury tightens my jaw, and I make a show of pulling out my phone, ready to dial 911. She panics. "Wait! I'm sorry."

"What are you sorry for?" Alice asks.

There's a tense silence.

"My girl asked you a question," I snap.

Cynthia takes a moment to compose herself, fury radiating from her body.

"I'm sorry if my remarks offended you." She spits the apology out like it's poison, hatred clouding her eyes.

The fucking nerve of this lady.

"You're going to have to do better than that," I say, glaring at her until she can no longer meet my gaze.

"Fine, I'm sorry for calling you useless." This time she says it woodenly, like she's reading from a script, refusing to meet Alice's gaze.

I start to pull Alice toward the door. "We're wasting our time here, baby," I say, loud enough for Cynthia to hear. "She's too proud to give you a genuine apology. She'll have plenty of time to reflect on it when she's locked in her cell."

My hand reaches for the door.

"I'm sorry!" she splutters. "I'll say sorry for anything you want. Just don't call the cops!"

I turn back toward her. She looks terrible: her eyes are crazed and her lips tremble.

"The problem is you're not sorry, Cynthia," I say. "You're sorry you were caught. And you'll say sorry if you think it will keep you out of jail. But you're not sorry."

There's a knock on the door. I've been expecting it. "Police, open up!" a voice shouts.

Cynthia squeaks, staring at the door in horror.

"I knew you wouldn't be sorry," I continue. "Which is why I got my brother to call the police before I came in. They're here to arrest you for theft." I reach to turn the handle. "Nobody hurts my girl and gets away with it. Especially not you."

Two police officers burst into the room, and Cynthia is cornered. She tries to dodge them and reach the door, but they're too quick for her. One of them slaps a pair of handcuffs on her wrists while the other tells her she has the right to remain silent. But she doesn't remain silent. She shrieks like a banshee, writhing and kicking as they pull her from the office and march her into the lobby.

"Go to hell, Mark Astor! Go to hell!" I hear her screech as they near the entrance doors.

Everyone stops and stares as she is dragged from the hotel, guests watching bemusedly at the scene unfolding before them. Employees whoop and cheer as Cynthia's screams are finally carried off in a police car, and Alice turns to me with a look of triumph on her face.

"You were amazing in there," I tell her.

"It felt so good to stand up for myself. It was even better than in my daydreams!" she says.

"I promised we'd fix it, baby. Cynthia will never be able to bully you again."

"I wonder what will happen to her." A flicker of worry crosses Alice's face. I can tell that she pities her ex-boss, despite everything. My baby has a heart of gold.

"She'll be fine. Don't worry about that."

Alice nods, taking a deep breath. "That was intense. Can we go back to your room? I want us to be alone." Her voice is so innocent, but I can see the naughty twinkle in her eye.

"That's the best plan I've heard all day."

I scoop her up bridal style, and she laughs as I carry her back to room 13.

9

———

ALICE

I NEVER DREAMED I could be so happy. I want to cry and laugh all at once as I'm carried to Mark's room. Cynthia is gone forever, and I'm in the arms of my dream man. Nothing could be better than this. I'm glowing like the sun, blissful, light shining from my every pore.

This must be what heaven feels like.

But this is only the beginning. Once we're in his bed, that's when heaven will really begin.

Mark opens the door to his room, still holding me with one brawny arm, and closes it behind us. It's getting dark outside, and the fire has been rekindled. A warm, cozy glow illuminates the room, making shadows dance on the four-poster bed.

Mark places me gently onto the mattress, easing himself on top of me.

"This time, you're not leaving this bed until I say so," he growls, pinning my arms above my head. His body traps mine. I'm powerless and totally at his mercy ... *and I love it.*

"Not even if the fire alarm goes off?" I tease.

"I'll fight the fucking fire myself if I have to. Nothing will stop me from making you mine this time, Alice." The tingling between my legs intensifies. I can feel the wetness pooling in my panties as he runs his hands over my body. "You're so sexy in your little uniform, but you'll be even sexier when it's off. I need to see you, baby."

He reaches a hand around my back to unzip my dress, unhooking my arms from the sleeves and pulling it down past my ankles until I'm lying in nothing but my wet panties.

Mark's eyes devour me, roaming over every inch of my skin. It takes him a moment to speak. "God, you're fucking perfect. Even more perfect than I imagined."

His hands grope my breasts, the soft flesh overflowing from his palms while he circles my hardened nipples with his fingers, making me shiver with pleasure. I moan as he sinks his mouth to my right nipple, teasing the hard pink bud with his tongue, alternating between light licks and intense sucking until I'm squirming and gasping for breath. It feels so good that I can hardly bear it. I pull on his hair as he sucks harder. *Yes!*

He pulls back from my nipple with a gentle tug and starts tracing feathery kisses down the flesh of my stomach, lower and lower, until he's blocked by my panties.

"Did you really think these sexy little things would keep me out?" Mark asks, cocking his head with a smirk.

I giggle, which turns into a gasp as he whips my panties down to my ankles, leaving me completely bare beneath his gaze. He eases my legs open and eyes my most intimate area, making me shiver as he stares hungrily at my raw nakedness. I've never felt so vulnerable ... so exposed. But somehow it feels right. It feels like this is exactly where I'm supposed to be: lying naked and help-less at Mark Astor's mercy.

His voice sounds strangled as he says, "You're so wet, baby. I need a taste."

A taste?

He sinks his head between my spread legs, his warm breath tickling the swollen nub of my clit. My hips buck wildly as his tongue slips between my slick folds, setting my nerves on fire.

"Yes, Mark!" I sob as his tongue circles my pussy, coating itself in my juices.

The world goes blank, and there is nothing but Mark's tongue, sliding relentlessly between my legs, dipping inside me as he laps up my arousal, making me squirm. He starts to lick upward until his mouth latches onto my engorged clit, sucking on it greedily until I can barely take it.

It's too much. It's too good.

Pressure builds inside me. It sinks from my abdomen down to my toes, blooming into a crescendo of clench-ing, tightening, until ...

"I'm going to come!" I cry.

The world explodes. My orgasm rockets through me, radiating from my pulsing pussy to every clenched muscle in my body until I'm quivering with pleasure. It doesn't stop until I'm panting, my hands still clawing at the sheets.

Mark watches me hungrily from between my legs, his lips wet with my arousal.

"Th-that was amazing," I say, still trembling. "I've never c-come so hard before."

He plants a kiss on my inner thigh. "I'm going to make you come again, baby. You better be ready."

I'm still weak and shaky from my orgasm, but I'm so ready for him. I'm agonizingly aware of the empty space inside me, aching to be filled with his cock. He's awakened a need in me that I never knew was there.

Mark eases off me, standing at the end of the bed, and I watch as he unbuttons his shirt to reveal his thick, muscly torso. My eyes are drawn to the trail of dark hair on his abdomen disappearing into his pants, which he quickly tugs down. I gulp. I can't help it. The outline of his erection strains against his boxers. It's so big. Impossibly big.

He yanks down the last piece of material separating us, and his huge cock springs free, thick and meaty, lined with bulging veins that make my eyes pop. A stream of pre-cum trickles from the tip, making the head glisten.

"This is going inside you," he says, his voice husky with need. "I'm going to make you feel so good, baby."

His words make me squirm with anticipation. But first, I want to taste him. Just like he tasted me. I shuffle to the edge of the bed, meeting Mark's gaze as I wrap my hand around the base of his cock, my fingertips not even close to meeting around his girth. The skin is soft around his hardness, like silk-covered steel, and I lower my head to gingerly lick the tip as Mark lets out a hiss of breath.

"Fuck, Alice."

He tastes musky and salty, like nothing I've ever tasted before.

This must be what sex tastes like.

I can't get enough. I take as much of him as I can into my mouth, my eyes watering as my lips stretch around him. His guttural moans spur me on. I bob my head up and down his shaft, moving faster and faster. *I'm sucking my man's cock.* It feels so deliciously naughty. My clit throbs, and I rub myself, trying to ease the aching need between my legs as I suck him.

Suddenly, Mark pulls out of my mouth, panting.

"Did I do something wrong?" I ask, my eyes wide.

He laughs hoarsely. "The opposite. It was too good, baby. I was getting too close." He pushes me back onto the bed, pinning my arms above my head. "I can't wait any longer. I need to be inside you."

He wrenches my legs apart and slides the tip of his cock between my folds, ready to thrust inside. A wave of panic hits me. *Will it hurt?*

"I've never done this before," I blurt out before he has a chance to push inside me.

He freezes, looking down at me like he doesn't dare to believe his ears. "You're a virgin?"

I nod, biting my lip. "Yes, but please don't stop! I really want this. I can learn, you can teach me, I can—"

Mark kisses me hard, cutting me off. I moan against

his lips, but it ends too soon, and there's a wild glint in his eyes as he pulls away.

"I am your first and your last. Do you understand? Nobody else will ever get to have you. Nobody else will get to kiss your lips or taste your pussy or make you come. Only me. Forever. Understood?"

I nod, melting at his words. It all sounds so right. There could never be anyone else—only Mark Astor. I'm his and he's mine. It's an undeniable truth, a fact of life that I feel in my bones. We are meant for each other, and I've known that somewhere inside me since the moment we met.

"Forever," I agree. "I love you, Mark."

"I love you too, Alice. And now, I'm going to show you just how much."

10

____

MARK

I FEEL like the luckiest guy in the whole fucking world. My girl is lying beneath me, her legs spread, looking up at me like I'm a god as she waits for me to take her virginity. She's so ripe for me. Her pussy is gushing, and part of me wants to lap it up so I can taste her sweet juices on my tongue again. But I can't wait another second. She's mine, and I'm ready to claim her.

Mine. It's the only thought echoing in my mind as I slowly ease my cock inside her. I feel her tense, her breath quickening as I push against the only barrier left between us. She gasps, her eyes screwing shut as I break through it and fill her pussy. Her walls squeeze my cock so hard it takes all my restraint not to come there and then. But I need to make this last. I need to make this perfect for her. She whimpers, opening her big brown eyes to stare up at me as I kiss her forehead.

"You're doing so good, baby. You're taking my cock like a good girl."

I pull out of her slowly before thrusting in again, a little faster this time.

"It's so big," Alice gasps, wriggling around as she tries to ease the discomfort.

"It's going to get better." I build up a gentle rhythm, easing in and out as her pussy clenches around my cock. Slowly, I see her start to relax. Her whimpers turn into soft moans, her eyes rolling back in pleasure. *She's ready.*

I pick up the pace, driving in and out of her pussy as her creamy juices gush onto my cock. Her moans grow louder as I move faster, the bed creaking beneath us as I fuck my girl hard.

"Yes!" she cries. "Oh God, yes! YES!"

She's writhing with pleasure, clawing at me like a wildcat as I pump in and out of her relentlessly. Our flesh slaps together, the sound mingling with our moans as I watch her breasts bounce up and down with every thrust.

"That's it," I bite out, my jaw clenched in concentration. "Take that cock, sweetie."

"Please," she whimpers. "Don't stop!"

Nothing in the world could stop me now.

I'm fucking her like an animal and she's meeting me with every thrust, jerking her hips back and forward to take me as deep as she can.

I want to see her ride me.

The thought is sudden and all-consuming. I pull out, smiling at Alice's desperate disapproval.

"Please," she begs. "I said don't stop. I need more ... I need you."

"Trust me, we're not stopping," I say. "I want you to ride me."

Alice's eyes go wide as I sit back on the bed. My rock-hard cock is coated in our juices, and I hold it in place, ready for her. She looks unsure, but straddles my lap and gingerly sinks down onto my cock with a loud moan, her face flushing with pleasure.

"Now, ride my dick until you come, baby," I command.

My girl knows when to do as she's told. She clings to me as she bounces up and down, crying out at the top of her lungs as she grinds her clit against me.

"It's so deep," she moans.

"You better get used to it. You're going to ride my cock like this every day for the rest of your life."

My words spur her on. She's bouncing even harder than before, her hips moving wildly.

She's so fucking hot.

I lean back to watch her little pussy sliding up and down, stretched tight around my bulging cock, covering it in her cream. Her moans intensify until she's wailing so loud the whole hotel can probably hear.

Good. I want them all to hear that she's mine.

I can feel her pussy clenching around me. Her eyes are glazing over. She's getting close.

"Come," I say. "Come on my dick, baby."

She claws desperately at my back and starts to scream, "YES! YES! YES!"

Her body convulses as the orgasm consumes her,

making her pussy pulse hard around my cock like it wants to milk me dry. I groan at the sensation, fighting back my own orgasm as my girl collapses on top of me, gasping, her body trembling with my dick still inside her.

"Don't think I'm done with you yet," I growl, pulling out of her and pushing her forward onto her knees facedown, her ass raised. "Now, I'm going to come inside you."

She gasps as I push into her pussy from behind, my cock disappearing between her thick, round ass cheeks. I spank them hard, making her whimper before I grab a fistful of her soft brown hair, pulling it taut as I start thrusting in and out of her once more.

"Oh, yes!" Alice moans as her body jerks back and forward with every thrust.

"You like that, baby?" I ask, my balls slapping hard against her clit.

"Yes! Come inside me, Mark."

I don't need to be asked twice. I grab her hips and let myself lose control. My heart hammers in my chest as I fuck my girl, raw and savage, groaning as my balls tighten and my cock starts to throb. *I want to fill her up.* With a deep moan, I bury my cock to the hilt and spurt a thick stream of cum inside her, coating her walls with my seed.

My girl, I think. *Mine.*

Alice squeezes her thighs together, trying to keep as much of my cum inside her as possible as I pull out.

"Good girl," I murmur, scooping her up in my arms and holding her tight. "You were perfect. So fucking perfect." *Better than perfect.*

She smiles up at me, her cheeks adorably flushed as she says, "That was way better than butterscotch pudding."

Chuckling, I kiss her gently, feeling the happiest I've ever been in my whole life. I can't believe that this perfect creature is mine, but she is. And I'm never letting her go.

11

ALICE

I NEVER IMAGINED sex would feel so good. My daydreams didn't even come close to the toe-curling plea-sure I just experienced with Mark. Thinking about it makes me grin like an idiot. The aching between my legs is finally gone, and I feel completely at peace as I lie in his arms, every muscle limp and relaxed.

I want to stay with him forever.

The thought hits me with a certainty that I've never felt before. I've spent my whole life unsure of myself—feeling scattered and confused—disappearing into the safety of my fantasies instead of seeking something real. In my head, everything is risk-free. I don't have to put myself out there or leave my comfort zone. But that's all my daydreams are. Dreams. And I want so much more than just dreams. I want something real—something forever.

And I think I've finally found it.

I shuffle closer to Mark, burying my face against his chest.

"I love you," I say, my voice muffled.

"I love you too." Hearing him say it so earnestly gives me a thrill of joy every time.

"Forever?"

"Longer than that," he says, smiling down at me. I try to smile back, but my mouth stretches into a yawn instead. "You tired?"

"Exhausted." My eyelids are growing heavy

He pulls me toward him, stroking my hair as I start to doze. "Get some rest, baby. Tomorrow is a very important day for us."

He sounds oddly mysterious, and I want to ask him what's so important about tomorrow, but the question is swallowed by sleep as it carries me under.

I WAKE UP EARLY. The sun has barely risen outside as I stretch out on the bed. The events of yesterday come rushing back in a joyful blur, and I turn toward Mark with a smile. But he's not there.

Frowning, I sit up and survey the room. The fire has turned to ash in the grate, leaving me feeling chillier than last night. I shiver as I get up, still naked, and pull on my uniform for warmth. Mark is nowhere to be seen, and I check every inch of the hotel room, starting to feel uneasy.

Where is he?

His clothes are still in the closet, and his toiletries are in the bathroom. I'm glad they are, otherwise I might think I daydreamed the whole thing.

Maybe he went down to the spa, or for a swim, or to ask for something at the reception desk.

I try to stay calm, convincing myself there's a reasonable explanation for why the man who took my virginity last night left before I woke up.

I start at the reception desk, where Jade is already busy at work.

"Hey Alice," she says brightly. "Didn't see you come in this morning. I assume you heard about Cynthia? Man, I always knew there was something wrong with that woman. She was a total snake! I'm so damn happy that she's gone. Do you remember that time when she —" I usually love chatting with Jade, but right now I can only think about Mark.

"Have you seen Mark Astor?" I cut in, my voice sounding strangely high-pitched.

"Uh, yeah, he went out first thing this morning. He seemed like he was in a hurry."

"When exactly did he leave?"

Jade shrugs, looking at the clock. "Like an hour ago, I guess."

"And he didn't say anything about where he was going?"

Jade leans across the desk conspiratorially. "Well, as it happens, I asked him about his plans for today. I mean, damn, when a man looks that good, he's worth making small talk for. He said something about going to

Burlington to see someone called Charlotte Monroe. He sounded pretty damn excited about it, too. Charlotte's a lucky girl, I tell you." She laughs.

I stare at her, feeling my insides turn to ice. "He said he was going to see a girl?"

"Sure did. A guy like that probably has dozens of them waiting in line ... what's got you so curious, anyway?" she asks, suddenly suspicious.

My mouth is so dry I can barely answer her. "Nothing, no reason. I just want to make sure he's enjoying his time here and not still thinking about closing us down."

It's the only excuse I can think of.

"Don't worry about that. With Cynthia gone, I'm sure this place will be back on track in no time." Jade gives me a winning smile, totally oblivious that my heart is crumbling in my chest.

I walk numbly back to room 13 before I realize that I don't have the keycard. I can't get back in. Slumping to the floor, I put my head in my hands and sob.

Is that it? I think. *Was it all a game? All lies?*

The pain is too much. I can't bear it. My imagination conjures up a million images of who Charlotte Monroe could be—some gorgeous rich girl, no doubt. I wrap my arms around myself, crying into my hands until a voice interrupts me.

"Alice?" I look up to see Mark striding down the corridor toward me. "Why are you sitting out here?" His face crumples when he sees my tears. "What's wrong, baby? Why are you crying?" He tries to pull me up into his arms, but I resist.

"Jade told me that you went to see a girl." My voice is thick and stuffy.

"What?" He looks bewildered.

I take a deep breath. "Jade works at reception. I woke up and you weren't there, and then Jade said you went to see a girl in Burlington. You left me first thing this morning to see another girl."

I dissolve into fresh sobs, feeling like the world's biggest idiot.

It was all too good to be true.

"Alice, listen to me," Mark says, crouching down so he's at my eye level. "You've got it all wrong. Come inside, and I'll explain everything." He wipes away my tears with his thumb, his face somber.

"But how can I trust you? I gave you everything, and it's like you couldn't wait to get away from me."

He recoils like I just slapped him. "Get away from you? That's literally the last thing I want. Being away from you for even a second is fucking hell for me."

He sounds so sincere. I desperately want to believe him. But before I can respond, he snatches me up in his arms and swipes his keycard, shouldering open the door to room 13 and carrying me inside.

"Mark!" I protest, but he doesn't release me until the door is closed behind us. He sets me down on the bed and starts rooting around behind the bedside table. "What are you doing?"

He doesn't answer until he finds what he's looking for: a piece of paper on the floor, partially hidden beneath the bed.

"I guess it got knocked off while you were asleep," he says, handing it to me. "Sorry, I should have put it somewhere safer."

Confused, I unfold the paper and start to read.

> *Dear Alice,*
>
> *Good morning, beautiful. I've gone to Burlington to get you something. It's a surprise, but hopefully a good one. Don't worry, I'll be back as soon as possible, hopefully before you wake up.*
>
> *I love you,*
> *Mark*

I read through it twice, my confusion deepening with every word.

"I don't understand. Jade said you were going to Burlington to meet a girl called Charlotte."

Mark's serious expression softens and he smiles at me, his eyes radiating so much love that my breath catches. I don't think I'll ever get used to how handsome he is.

"Yes," he says. "I went to see Charlotte Monroe. But she's an eighty-year-old woman, not a girl."

What?

"But who *is* Charlotte Monroe?"

Mark sits down beside me, taking my hands in his. "Charlotte Monroe is a jeweler. One of the best in the country. She lives over in Burlington, and she's an old family friend, so I paid her a visit. I wanted to buy something from her."

"What did you want to buy?" I ask.

Mark takes a deep breath. His eyes are fixed on mine, and my heart starts to pound.

"A ring," he says.

I watch in awe as he sinks down on one knee and pulls a small black ring box from his suit pocket. Time slows down as he opens it to reveal a glittering diamond ring. I gape at him, my whole body trembling with joy.

Oh my God!

Mark grins at me and asks, "Alice, will you marry me?"

MARK

I WATCH as Alice glows with joy, her sadness forgotten as she stares down at the ring in my hand. It was almost impossible to leave her this morning—she looked so damn beautiful curled up naked in my bed—but I knew I couldn't wait another second to officially make her mine. So I left as early as possible to go to Burlington and buy Charlotte Monroe's most beautiful diamond ring. Only the best for my Alice.

"I know it's sudden, and maybe you think I'm crazy," I say, my heart thumping hard against my ribs, "but I fell in love with you the moment I saw you. And I want to make you my wife, Alice. I want to spend the rest of my life with you. I love you."

Her hands cover her mouth. "I can't believe this is happening," she gasps, happy tears streaming down her face. "Yes, I will marry you! A million times, yes. I love you so much, Mark."

I'm fucking ecstatic as I slide the ring onto her finger

and pull her close, my lips crashing down to meet hers. *She's mine! Forever!* I want to shout it triumphantly from the rooftops so everyone knows. *God help any man who forgets it.*

"There's one more thing I want to say," I tell her, pulling away and taking her hands in mine. "I know it's been hard for you to trust that I'm not going to abandon you ..."

"Oh Mark," she says, running her fingers through my hair. "You just asked me to marry you! I trust you completely. I'm so sorry I ever doubted you."

"You don't need to apologize, baby. I'm glad you trust me, but there's still one more thing I want to do to show you how serious I am about you. About us."

She stares at me with wide-eyed curiosity as I pull my phone from my pocket and turn it on. I dial my brother's number, and he answers immediately.

"Mark, what the hell is going on?" Daniel bellows. "I get some cryptic text from you saying I have to call the cops on Cynthia Ratcliff, then I hear nothing from you for nearly twenty-four fucking hours. Care to explain what the fuck is happening?"

"The cops came and they arrested her," I say simply.

"But—"

"I'll go over it with you later, Daniel. That's not why I called."

"Well, why did you call then, dickwad? To get me to call the cops on someone else? Hell, why don't we get all our employees arrested? That'll be great for business!"

His voice is laced with angry sarcasm. My brother has always had a pretty short fuse.

"I called to tell you I'm stepping down as CEO."

Dead silence. Alice is goggling at me, and I give her a wink. It takes my brother a long time to finally speak.

"What the fuck are you talking about?"

"I can't make it any clearer, Daniel. I'm stepping down as CEO, and I want you to take over the Astor chain."

"Have you gone fucking insane?" he splutters.

"I've never been saner, buddy. Besides, it's the job you've always wanted. I know you'll make a damn good CEO."

Daniel makes a noise of disbelief. "I don't get it. You love this job. It's been your whole life for years. Why the hell are you giving it up now?"

I smile and look at Alice: my beautiful girl, with her soft lips and sexy body and big brown eyes full of love for me. The answer couldn't be clearer. "I've found something more important."

"But—"

"Don't worry, we'll work out all the admin and make it official as soon as possible," I interrupt. "Right now, though, I'm going to shut off my phone and spend some time with my fiancée."

"Your fiancée?! What the fu—"

I chuckle as I hang up on him mid-sentence. *Damn right, my fiancée.*

Alice leaps into my arms, smothering me with kisses, laughing blissfully as I pick her up and spin her around.

"I can't believe you did that for me," she says, beaming up at me. "Are you sure this is what you want?"

"I've never been surer of anything in my life."

"But your company—"

"It's in good hands, baby. Besides, I can still work for the Astor if I need to. I'll just work from home so I can be with you." Alice looks like she could burst with happiness as she cocoons herself in my arms.

This decision feels so natural. So right. What does being CEO of the Astor matter if I don't have my girl? What's the point of working all the time if I'm not really happy? Of being rich if I can't spoil the woman I love? Nothing in the world could ever be more important than her.

"What happens now?" Alice asks, still looking dazed with bliss. "Where are we going to live? Your apartment in New York?"

"We're going to live wherever you want, baby. I don't care where I live as long as it's with you."

"Really? Anywhere I want?"

I smile at her. "Where do you daydream about living?"

"All sorts of places," she says, grinning with excitement. "A lake house, a cozy log cabin, a quaint English cottage, a penthouse, a medieval castle ..." I kiss her nose. Her enthusiasm is so cute. And so sexy.

"Sounds like we have a lot of options to choose from. But first, there's something even more important we have to handle."

"What's that?"

I pounce. She gasps as I scoop her up and throw on her the bed, pinning her beneath me.

"We haven't made our engagement official," I say.

She squirms as I push my growing erection against her, making her gasp.

"That's definitely something that needs to be fixed," she moans.

"Oh, you bet I'm going to fix it, Mrs. Astor."

Alice's eyes light up. "Mrs. Astor ... I like the sound of that."

"Me too, baby," I say. "Me too."

EPILOGUE 1
ALICE

SUNLIGHT STREAMS through the window as I wake up slowly, snuggling against my husband's warm, naked body.

"Good morning, beautiful," he says, his voice husky with sleep.

I smile. "Good morning."

I shuffle out of bed and pause in front of the window to stretch, admiring the lake as it glitters beneath the morning sun.

The last three years with Mark have been better than all my fantasies put together. We lived out so many of my dreams, from swimming with dolphins in Hawaii to riding in a hot-air balloon over Cappadocia. Our experiences made me feel so alive. It was a crazy whirlwind of adventure, and getting to do it all with the love of my life was a dream come true. But eventually, I started to miss Vermont. I wanted somewhere I could feel grounded, and I guess there really is no place like home. So Mark bought us a huge lake house, right on Lake Champlain, where we spend our days enjoying each other in every possible way.

Mark still works for the Astor, but he does it from home, allowing us to spend as much time together as possible. His new hours are short and flexible, finally giving him time to explore his love of cooking. The kitchen is his favorite room in the house, after our bedroom, of course, and he's often in there for hours at a time, whipping up the most delicious meals for us both.

As for me, I've been channeling my daydreams into paintings, trying to make something tangible and beautiful from my fantasies. It's a work in progress, but I'm learning fast and I'm proud of how far I've come.

I think I'll always be a daydreamer. It's part of me. But it's no longer because I have anything bad to escape from in my real life. Because real life is wonderful. Waking up next to my gorgeous man every morning fills me with joy, and every day with him is even better than the last. He's my home.

"Where do you think you're going?" he growls as I turn away from the window.

He reaches out and pulls me back into bed with him, trailing kisses down my body. I never used to be a morning person—waking up early was just a necessity for work—but morning sex with Mark has changed that. Waking up early is a pleasure now.

He descends on my pussy immediately, his mouth greedy as he laps up my arousal, getting me ready for him.

He's already rock-hard, just like every morning. My husband is insatiable.

When he can't wait any longer, he slides inside me in one slow movement, his hips rocking lazily back and forth, savoring every stroke as I tip my head back and moan for him. The slow pace doesn't last long—my moans bring out the animal in him and soon he's fucking me hard, pounding me until I'm screaming and coming all over his cock, the bed creaking beneath us.

Yeah, mornings are pretty damn great now.

He comes inside me with a guttural groan, and warm contentment spreads from my head to my toes. Today is going to be a good day. It always is with Mark.

"I've been thinking ..." he says once our breathing has returned to normal.

"What about?"

He looks at me, his intense gaze still enough to make my breath catch. "About family."

I can't stop the smile from spreading across my face.

I've been expecting this. The subject of children came up early on in our marriage, but I didn't feel ready yet. I wanted time with my husband—just me and him having adventures together. So, I kept taking the pill. But now that we've finally slowed down and built a stable life in Vermont, I've been revisiting my decision. We have a beautiful home and a lot of love to give. I think it's time we share it.

"I've been thinking about it too," I say. "And I'm ready."

Mark's eyes light up, his face splitting into a grin.

"Oh baby, you have no idea how much I was hoping you'd say that." His smile is contagious.

"I can't wait to have a family with you."

"Me neither," he says. "So let's not wait another second."

I giggle as he pins my arms above my head, sinking his mouth to my neck and leaving a trail of hungry kisses. I'm still wet from our first round, and he wastes no time slipping his huge length back inside me, making me pant with desire.

"I'm going to fill you up with our babies."

"That sounds like a great plan," I say before my husband starts to fuck me, and all coherent speech is replaced with the sound of our desperate moans.

Heaven, I think. *This is heaven.*

EPILOGUE 2
MARK

THE ART GALLERY is heaving with people. Alice wasn't expecting a big turnout, but I'm not surprised that so many people are here. My wife's talent never ceases to amaze me.

"Where's Mom?" my son, Noah, asks as he peers around the gallery.

He's tall for a nine-year-old and has my vivid blue eyes. I ruffle his hair and point toward Alice, who is standing in front of her best-known painting, *The Green Mountain Nymphs*, greeting people as they admire her creations. Her hand rests against her swollen belly, and I get a fierce urge to carry her home, away from all these people, where I know she'll be safe. But I don't. I know what today means for my wife.

Ever since she discovered her love of painting, Alice's career as an artist has slowly flourished. She paints the landscapes of Vermont with her own dreamy flair, adding mythical creatures and fantasy elements to her work.

Each painting feels like a vivid daydream, and people love it. After years of hard work, Alice Astor is finally becoming a big name in the art world, and I'm so damn proud of her.

"I want to see Mommy," Emily, my daughter, whines.

At the age of four, Emily is my wife in miniature, from the freckles on her nose to her pretty brown eyes.

"Okay sweetie, let's go see Mommy."

I guide the kids toward Alice, who beams when she spots us and weaves her way through the crowd to reach us.

"Mommy!" Emily says, throwing herself into my wife's arms. Alice squeezes her tight, grinning up at me.

"There are tons of people here, baby," I say. "Your exhibition's a hit."

Alice blushes. "I know. I can't believe it! I was worried nobody would come."

"But we came!" Emily says eagerly. She's a mommy's girl through and through.

"I know, sweetie. I can always count on you," Alice says. "Are you guys hungry? There's a snack table near the back."

"Where?" Noah asks, whipping his head around.

He's a slender kid, but my son sure likes his food.

Alice points out the table and Emily chimes in, "I'm hungry, too."

"I'll take Emily to get snacks," Noah says, straightening up like a grown-up. He's always trying to prove that he's responsible.

"Okay, but come straight back," I order as Noah

takes his sister's hand and makes a show of guiding her carefully through the crowd.

"He's so protective," Alice muses, closing the space between us as she wraps her arms around me. "Just like his dad."

"I'm only protective of what's mine," I say, resting my forehead against hers. "Like you."

"I know. It's sexy." She's whispering in my ear now, her body pressed against mine, making my cock swell. "I'm all yours, Mark."

"You bet you are, baby. And when we get home tonight, I'm going to prove it."

And I will. My wife captivates me more and more every day, and my love for her has only grown stronger with time. I'm so fucking glad I met her because I can't imagine life without her or our two perfect babies. Soon to be three. They are everything to me.

My dad's motto was "Are you ready to work harder than yesterday?". But I'm not my dad. My motto is "Are you ready to love harder than yesterday?". And when I look at my beautiful wife, I know the answer will always be yes.

CONTINUE THE SERIES
THE CEO ON FLOOR 76

THE CEO ON FLOOR 76
LAYLA

It's a sweltering day in Manhattan. I'm surprised my shoes don't stick to the sidewalk as I head toward the imposing Astor Tower, droplets of sweat running down my forehead. My makeup is definitely ruined.

Not the best start to my first day at work.

I still can't believe I'm actually here. Only a month ago, I was still living with my mom in our tiny shoebox house in Tennessee, working as a receptionist for an equally tiny newspaper company. Now I'm in New York City on the hottest day of the year, and I'm desperately trying to look like I belong here.

A yellow cab zooms past me, way too close, and I pick up the pace, not wanting to get flattened by one of New York's crazy drivers before I even get to work.

Astor Tower dwarfs the surrounding buildings. It's all smooth steel and black glass, gleaming like gunmetal in the sunlight. I step through the revolving doors and sigh with relief at the gloriously crisp air conditioning inside. It's like walking into the freezer aisle at the grocery store.

The entrance is a sprawling expanse of shiny white floors and people in suits rushing around, all looking busy and intimidating.

What the hell am I doing here?

I've been asking myself that question all morning.

Mentally pulling myself together, I head to the elevator and hit the button for floor 76.

Top floor.

Getting to work at the top of Astor Tower is going to be insane, and I feel a flutter of excitement in my chest as I imagine looking out at New York City every morning. It's what I'm most looking forward to about this job. But being a personal assistant is definitely not my dream, especially not for some bigshot CEO like Daniel Astor, who apparently has a reputation for flying off the handle.

I haven't actually met my new boss yet. His HR manager, Tyler, interviewed me and gave me the job. It was Tyler who mentioned Daniel's temper, and even though the thought of having an angry boss made me apprehensive at first, I'm starting to think it's probably a good thing.

I don't want a nice boss.

Sounds crazy, I know. But more specifically, I don't want a boss I can fall in love with—not after everything that happened back in Tennessee. I'll happily take Daniel Astor and his anger management issues over any of that crap.

I feel nauseous as the elevator ascends. Despite

keeping it together all morning, the nerves are finally getting to me, and I don't want to reach the top. I could leave right now. I could hop on a plane back to Tennessee and write this off as a crazy idea.

No, I tell myself firmly. *Be brave.*

All too soon, the doors open, and I'm standing in a giant, open-plan office where hundreds of people sit staring at computers. It's surprisingly quiet, aside from the tap-tap-tap of keyboards. Nobody notices me, and I don't know whether to be relieved or disappointed at the lack of welcome. In Tennessee, there were only ten of us at the newspaper company. It was tight-knit. Clearly, Astor Tower isn't that kind of place.

That's a good thing, I remind myself. *You don't want things to be like they were in Tennessee.*

Still, I need someone to show me what the hell I'm meant to be doing.

There's a group of employees standing around a coffee machine, muttering to each other—or more specifically, gossiping. I approach them nervously.

"Excuse me," I say, ready to ask them where I need to go.

They turn to look at me and I recognize one of them as Tyler, the guy who interviewed me. He's probably in his mid-twenties, but his baby face and clean-shaven jaw make him look more like a teenager.

"Hello Layla," he says, his face stretching into a grin. "Welcome to Astor Tower."

"Thank you. It's good to be here." *Sort of.*

Tyler gestures to the people around him. "This is

Claire, Juan, and Toni, all from accounts. Guys, this is Layla."

I shake all their hands, plastering a fake smile on my face.

Relax, I think. *Be friendly. Be cool.*

"Nice to meet you, Layla," Claire says. "Which department do you work for?"

Tyler cuts in before I can answer. "Layla is Mr. Astor's new PA." He says it like he's just revealed an especially juicy piece of gossip, and it certainly gets the group's attention. They're all staring at me with renewed interest.

"Wow, good luck taming that beast," Toni says, her eyebrows raised. "You've got your work cut out for you."

I laugh nervously like it's a joke, but they all look dead serious. It's doing nothing to help my nerves.

Is it too late to make a break for the elevator?

"Let me show you to Mr. Astor's office," Tyler says.

He leads me all the way to the back of the main office toward a wooden door with an inscribed gold plaque:

Mr. Daniel Astor

Chief Executive Officer

Tyler knocks.

My heart starts to beat faster as I hear an angry grunt and heavy footsteps from inside. I'm half expecting a giant to burst through the door and eat me whole. Then it opens, and Daniel Astor stands before us. He might not be a giant, but he's not far off: he towers more than a foot above my five-foot-two frame, his broad shoulders filling the doorway. My heart sinks as I look up at him.

He's handsome. Devilishly, panty-droppingly handsome, with a long straight nose, a chiseled jaw dotted with stubble, and deep green eyes that are fixed angrily on Tyler.

"What?" he snaps.

"Sorry to disturb you, Mr. Astor," Tyler says. "This is Layla White. She's the new PA I hired."

Those breathtaking green eyes land on me, and my breath catches. The power of his gaze is suffocating, and my cheeks redden as he takes in my plus-size figure. I feel so naked. *But I like it?* My body betrays me, my nipples hardening and straining against my blouse. I'm already captivated by this man ... already turned on by him.

Oh boy, this isn't good.

"She's my new PA?" Daniel asks in his growly voice. He sounds so shocked that for a moment, I feel self-conscious. I tug at my black pencil skirt, trying to smooth it out over my curves.

"Yes, sir," Tyler says. He's frowning, no doubt worried that he's pissed off his boss by hiring me.

Mr. Astor is still staring at me, incredulous, his eyes darkening with something I can't put my finger on. His surprise is starting to worry me. Why is it so shocking that I'm his new PA? Why is he looking at me like he can't believe his eyes?

"I have experience," I squeak, my voice an octave higher than usual. "It's all on my resumé."

"Yes!" Tyler says, latching onto my comment like it's a life preserver. "It's a good resumé, Mr. Astor. I can send it to you straight away if you want to check it over yourself. She was our youngest candidate, but she's very eager to advance her career and already has some solid experience." He's talking like someone is holding a gun to his head, and I can't help but feel a tug of annoyance when he mentions me being young. I may only be twenty, but I look my age. Tyler looks about fifteen.

Daniel clearly isn't listening—he's too busy looking at me. His eyes never once leave my face as he curtly tilts his head at Tyler. This is apparently Tyler's cue to get lost because he scurries away as quickly as possible. Part of me wants him to come back. I feel like I've been left alone with a lion.

A hungry lion.

"Come in," Daniel says, opening the door to his office.

I can hear in his voice that it's not a request; it's an order. I take a deep breath and do as he says.

Continue Reading
www.books2read.com/astoralphas2

Claimed by the Lumberjack

Loved by the Lumberjack

Wanted by the Lumberjack

Rescued by the Lumberjack

Frozen Peak

A Mountain Man for Christmas

The Mountain Man's Second Chance

The Mountain Man's Forbidden Love

A Mountain Man for Valentine's Day

The Mountain Man's Fake Girlfriend

The Mountain Man's Curvy Pen Pal

Collections

Snowfall Ridge (Books 5-8)

Snowfall Ridge (Books 1-4)

Blaze Valley Ranch (Books 1-5)

Wildwood Forest (Books 1-4)

Frozen Peak (Books 1-6)

Clara King writes short and steamy romance books featuring grumpy heroes who are tough on the outside and gooey on the inside. Her heroines are strong, curvy women with big dreams and sunshine personalities. Clara's books include age gaps, cozy small towns, and a happy ending for every couple.

When she's not writing, Clara can be found reading, watching comedies, and eating anything remotely chocolate-based. She's a history nerd, a cat person, and a fan of all things Jane Austen.

www.authorclaraking.com

www.ingramcontent.com/pod-product-compliance
Lightning Source LLC
Chambersburg PA
CBHW020351160726
47987CB00022BA/2511